The Empty Place

a child's guide

through grief

by Roberta Temes Ph.D
illustrations by Kim Carlisle

SMALL HORIZONS
Far Hills, New Jersey

Library of Congress Catalog Card Number: 92-60613

Dr. Roberta Temes
The Empty Place

ISBN 0-88282-118-0
SMALL HORIZONS
A Division of New Horizon Press
1997 / 5 4 3 2

DEDICATED TO DAVID

In my family there
is an empty place.

There is an empty place
in the kitchen,

in the backyard,

even in the car.

Sometimes I feel
an empty place
inside me, too.

When I feel empty,
the emptiness is in
the middle of my heart.

Some days
I am a regular,
ordinary third grader.

But some days,
I feel sad,
or I feel lonely,
or I feel sorry,

or I feel scared.

or I feel angry.

I feel sad,
because Jennifer
is dead!

I feel lonely,
because now I
have no sister.

I feel sorry,
because last Thanksgiving
Jennifer gobbled up
all my turkey stuffing.
So I punched her
really hard
and she cried
really loud.

I feel angry,
because nobody
has time for me any more.
Our house
is much too quiet.

I feel scared,
because some day
my mother could
die or my father
could die,

or I could die.

My baby sitter, Betsy, told me she used to have two brothers. Now she has one, because one of them died. His name was Todd. He didn't die from a serious sickness, like Jennifer did. He died because of a car accident.

Betsy said that after Todd died she had empty feelings, too. She used to feel empty in her stomach. These days Betsy isn't empty any more.
Betsy thinks my friends will start coming here again. When they do, we'll flip baseball cards, and play monster, and do homework if Mom says we have to. Maybe then I won't feel so empty.

Betsy said that she used to feel sad and cry, especially at bedtime. These days Betsy isn't sad anymore. She plays with Todd's games and she looks at pictures of him and she listens to his records. She put Todd's books in her bookcase, except for the dinosaur books. Betsy thinks dinosaurs are gross.

Betsy thinks it's O.K. for me to go into Jennifer's room. I can use her tape recorder and I can remember how nice she was. She was fun. I miss her. I'll look at the school pictures on her wall. Maybe then I won't feel so sad.

Betsy has one brother who didn't die, but she used to feel lonely for Todd anyway. These days Betsy feels lonely just a little bit. Most of the time she reads books, or watches T.V., or talks on the phone, or does her homework, or goes to gymnastic class, or baby-sits for me!

Betsy said that when she was feeling very lonely, right after Todd died, she had a lot to talk about. She talked to her mother, and her father, and her brother, and even her goldfish!

Betsy thinks I'll have a new brother or sister some day. I hope so.
But, if we don't get a new baby maybe we'll get a dog. I would love a basset hound. I would walk it, and feed it, and brush it, and train it.

Maybe then
I won't feel so lonely.

Betsy told me that her science teacher explained that everybody has germs, and most people get sick and then get all better. Betsy told me that at lunch-time in her school plenty of kids fight with each other, and punch each other, and make each other cry. None of them die. Maybe I shouldn't have punched Jennifer in the belly that time, but that's not what made her die, anyway.

Betsy was real angry when Todd died because every-
thing changed. Her parents became grouches. Her
grandparents became cry-babies. Sometimes her father stayed in his bed for days and days. Sometimes
her mother hollered at everyone for no reason. Betsy
is not angry anymore. Her mother and father sometimes are sad, but after the sadness comes a smile.

Betsy thinks my family may go on a vacation during the summer. And then my mother and father will joke around with me, just like before Jennifer died. They'll read me stories, and tell me knock-knock jokes. Jokes like,

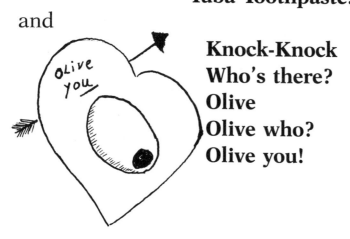

Knock-Knock
Who's there?
Tuba
Tuba who?
Tuba Toothpaste!

and

Knock-Knock
Who's there?
Olive
Olive who?
Olive you!

And then they'll ask me Silly-Head riddles, too. Riddles like,

Why did the Silly-Head take a ladder to school?
Because he wanted to be in High School!
and
Why did the Silly-Head policeman arrest the base-ball player?
Because the ballplayer stole some bases!

Maybe when we tell jokes again in my family, I won't feel so angry.

Betsy used to feel scared just like I do. She would run into her parents' bedroom every morning to be sure they didn't die during the night. She doesn't do that anymore. She doesn't feel scared anymore. Well, maybe sometimes.

Betsy knows that soon I won't have all these terrible feelings all day long.

Betsy thinks I should ask my mother and my father to buy me a new notebook.

I will print in it and I will color in it. (Next year it won't be printing anymore. Do you know why? Because fourth grade is script!)

Whenever I have a thought about Jennifer, I'll write it in my Jennifer notebook.

Whenever I have a feeling about Jennifer I'll draw it in my Jennifer notebook.

I will keep my
Jennifer notebook forever.
Even when I am very old.
Even when I am twenty.

The End